LOVE THE WORLD

TODD PARR

Megan Tingley Books
LITTLE, BROWN AND COMPANY
NEW YORK BOSTON

Also by Todd Parr

A complete list of Todd's books and more information can be found at toddparr.com.

About This Book

The art for this book was created on a drawing tablet using an iMac, starting with bold black lines and dropping in color with Adobe Photoshop. This book was edited by Megan Tingley and Allison Moore and designed by Nicole Brown and Saho Fujii. The production was supervised by Erika Schwartz, and the production editor was Marisa Finkelstein. The text was set in Todd Parr's signature font.

Love the world.

Love your face.

Love your space.

Love your nose.

Love your toes.

Love your eyes.

Love your size.

Love your walk.

Love giving a hand.

Love taking a stand.

LOVE

LOVE THE

YOURSELF.

WORLD!

Love the bees.

Love the trees.

Love your ears.

I FEEL BETTER!

Love your tears.

Love your hair.

BAA!

BAA!

Love your flair.

Love being kind.

Goodbye!

Love using your mind.

Love making art.

Love sharing your heart.

HEE HA HA
HEE

Love your giggle.

Love your wiggle.

Love your grin.   Love your skin.

Love the land.

Love the sea.

Love the earth.

Love you and me.

LOVE

LOVE THE

YOURSELF.
WORLD!

You will meet many people and go to many places. You can always find something to love about yourself, the world, and everyone in it. Love yourself, and love the world. The End. LOVE, Todd